I0621421

Sabrina's Storm

A NOVELLA

CB SAMET

AVANTSTAR
PUBLISHING

cbsamet.com

This is a work of fiction. Names, characters, places and incidents either are the product of the author's imagination or are used fictitiously, and any resemblance to any actual persons, living or dead, events, or locales is entirely coincidental.

Cover Design by: GET COVERS

Paperback ISBN: 978-1-950942-60-2

A ROMANCING THE
SPIRIT NOVELLA

SABRINA'S STORM

CB SAMET

Praise For CB SAMET

Four-time award winning author

"... women engagingly contend with otherwordly entities and real-world danger, while also grappling with that most mysterious phenomena: the human heart. Samet's prose vacillates skillfully between various registers, expressing sensuality, suspense, and humor, as needed.

A collection of well-executed ... tales of love and ghosts."

— KIRKUS REVIEWS (ON ROMANCING THE SPIRIT SERIES, NOVELLAS 1-6)

"[Romancing the Spirit Series: books 1-7] packs an emotional punch, with vivid characters, well-thought-out plots, and unusual paranormal twists."

— JAMIE BEE (BOOKBUB REVIEWER)

One

Gray autumn clouds rolled across a high sun, framing the three-story beach house with faded wood paneling. Porch steps led up to a weathered, baby-blue door. Behind the house, sand dunes stretched to the ocean with beach grass swaying in the salty breeze.

The secluded bed and breakfast made a pleasant vacation spot. Too bad Grant Dalton wasn't visiting for vacation. He had a job to do, but he would wait to move his equipment discreetly inside after he toured the house and met the owner.

With his suitcase by his side, he knocked on the door. No answer. He checked his watch, noting he'd arrived forty-five minutes early. He fished in his pocket, withdrew his phone, and checked his email. The rental instructions included the key code in case he came early or if the owner was out of the vicinity.

He punched in the code, which unlocked a key holder. With the key, he let himself inside the house.

"Hello?"

No answer came, but the chandelier in the dining room to his left shuddered as if opening the door had created a stiff breeze.

Curious, he thought.

No lights were on, but sunlight shone through the windows on either side. Yet the house still felt shadowy—dim and a bit lonely. The dark, stained floors and wood wall paneling made the foyer seem small, but the aged wood looked restored.

He'd spent time in creepy, dilapidated houses. This one was cared for, though he'd expected as much based on the online photos. Still, the decor lacked warmth or personal touches—pictures, paintings, or even a bouquet of flowers. So, it neither felt warm and cozy like a beach rental house, nor appeared decrepit and worn like a haunted house.

Grant carried his luggage up the stairs, first door on the left, to his rented room. Now *this* was a bed and breakfast room. Oak framed paintings of beaches and ships at sea hung on sky-blue walls.

One acrylic in particular caught his eye—a ship with an albatross soaring overhead. He wondered if it had been inspired by *The Rime of the Ancient Mariner*. He knew the poem well from a paper he'd written ten years ago in college English.

> *The ship was cheered, the harbour cleared,*
> *Merrily did we drop*
> *Below the kirk, below the hill,*
> *Below the lighthouse top.*

The bedspread was forest green with compasses and nautical ropes. A dozen plump, decorative pillows lay at the head of the bed.

Interesting. Maybe the owner had some type of pillow fetish.

A desk and chair against one wall held a small envelope. He opened it and read the note.

Thank you for staying at Oceanside Bed and Breakfast. Breakfast is served daily at eight am and dinner at six pm. Please give me a day's advance notice if you need different meal times. Clean towels are in the bathroom. The desk can be moved onto the balcony during the day for writing inspiration.
Sincerely, your host,
Sabrina Morningstar

He admired the penmanship and personal touch. She'd remembered he'd listed the purpose of his 'vacation' as writing time. He hadn't lied—he did need time to write. He hoped to put pen to paper (or fingers to keyboard) while he was here, but personal writing wasn't his primary objective.

Sabrina wouldn't know his true purpose until the opportune time—on camera. On that note, he needed to get his video equipment out of his vehicle discretely while no one else was there. But maybe he could take a moment to enjoy the balcony view. One of the joys of his job was traveling, so he was sure to enjoy the scenery. Few places he'd visited had such a splendid view as this.

He stepped outside to a pleasant October ocean breeze. Beneath a now completely overcast sky, the water was a choppy sapphire. The beach sloped up toward the house, and a sun-bleached gray walkway bridged the erosion dune to connect house and beach. In the backyard, a raised garden grew squash, cauliflower, lettuce, and Brussel sprouts.

With the wind in his hair and salt on his tongue, Grant realized this was probably the nicest 'haunted' house he'd ever stayed in. Too bad he'd never stay again. Once he revealed peoples' fraudulent claims of their tourist-trap houses harboring ghosts, people tended to want to never see him again. Some even went as far as restraining orders and threats. He wasn't sure why—he wasn't the criminal in these scenarios.

The beach had been deserted until Grant noticed a jogger. A woman with short platinum blonde hair kept close to the surf, running in the compact sand but still leaving a trail of prints. She appeared to be close to his age, about thirty. She stopped at the beach parallel to the house and began to strip.

He took a step back and glanced nervously around. He wasn't voyeuristic, and this woman obviously thought she was relaxing alone. When he glanced back in her direction, his tension eased as he noticed her white swimsuit against tan skin. She had an hour-glass figure, drawing his eyes to a narrow waist and muscular thighs.

She pulled a kayak from the beach into the surf. After wading hip deep into the water, she climbed in the boat and began paddling. He shuddered for her—the water was probably sixty-five degrees, but maybe the coolness felt refreshing after a long run.

Had it been a long run? He looked up and down the beach, wondering where she'd come from and if she lived nearby or visited on vacation.

Didn't matter. He wasn't here to meet a woman. Not exactly. He was here to expose a fraud—Sabrina Morningstar.

SABRINA TOWELED OFF and sat on the beach after her paddling. The waves had given her a robust workout. Resting back on her elbows, she watched the slate clouds moving briskly overhead. The vast Atlantic Ocean churned before her. She loved the expanse of it—water as far as the eye could see with no buildings obstructing the view.

She could look into the ocean for hours and feel small and insignificant. Doing so made her problems feel small and insignificant as well. When she mentally shrank them to a manageable size in this way, they fit nicely into something the size of a small jewelry box she could lock away until they outgrew their prison once again.

When her phone rang, she fished it out of her shorts pocket in the pile of clothes beside her. "Hi, Lee Ann."

"Sabrina, how are you?" her sister asked.

"I'm good. What's up?"

Sabrina recognized her sister's familiar patterns. If she launched into her day at work, then Sabrina knew she wanted casual conversation. If Lee Ann opened with a question, then she was all business.

"It's mid-October. We haven't heard if you're coming to Thanksgiving this year."

"I'm not sure. I might get a late renter." Truthfully, Sabrina wasn't sure she possessed the emotional fortitude for a large family gathering. Half of them would know what happened—or some version of a passed around story. They'd give her wide berth with looks of pity. The other half wouldn't know her story and so would ask her how a job she didn't have any more was treating her.

Not good. Not good at all.

"Well, Mom's up my butt to find out if you're coming. What do you want me to tell her?"

Her mom would set her younger sister to pester her.

"Tell her I don't yet know." Sabrina could know. She could simply mark the dates on the online rental calendar as 'unavailable.' But since she kept dumping money into the beach house repairs, she needed rentals.

Maybe the writer coming today would find inspiration and stay longer. After all, he'd insisted on renting all three bedrooms so he could have the peace and quiet he desired. Odd, since peace and quiet waited a short walk away at the beach, but because he was paying, she wasn't going to tell him what to do. Also, one person meant smaller meals to fix, and therefore a smaller grocery bill for the 'all-inclusive' meal part of her bed and breakfast.

"Sabrina?"

"Yeah?"

"You have to let it go." Lee Ann's voice was part pleading, part demanding.

If only letting go of the past was so simple. "I'm trying."

"Just decide to let it go, and then it will be gone."

"Like flipping a switch?" Sabrina's question came out harsher than she'd intended.

"It's been over a year," her sister pressed.

Three hundred seventy-two days to be exact. Three hundred seventy-two days Sabrina had stolen from Patrick's life.

"I'm trying," she repeated.

She said goodbye, disconnected the call, and headed back toward the house, carrying her kayak and paddle.

GRANT ENJOYED the sea breeze until a sudden grating noise behind him had him spinning around. The glass balcony door slid shut.

"What the—?" He tried to pull it back open, but the latch wouldn't budge. He looked through the glass into the room but saw no one.

His heart pounded until he took a few deep breaths to steady himself. He'd been trapped inside spooky rooms more times than he could count. No cause for alarm. He tugged on the door again. This was a convincing trick—no doubt engineered to maintain the illusion of a haunted house.

He banged on the door a few times, feeling his irritation mount. But unleashing his frustration on the glass door wasn't going to budge the lock, so he reined in his temper.

Moving away from the sliding door, he looked over the balcony. He could climb the rail and lower himself down to the first-floor balcony, but he wasn't certain the rail would hold his weight as he clung to it. He was stuck waiting for the hostess to return home.

"Please don't jump. You'll only hurt yourself," a female voice said.

He whirled around to the open balcony door where a woman stood—the same woman from the beach. She had a round face with dark blue eyes, like stormy waters, rimmed in dark mascara. She wore a silver necklace and the same running clothes he'd seen her in on the beach. Her choppy blond hair stopped at her ears and was still damp.

"Mr. Dalton?" she asked.

He cleared his throat. "Yes. And you are?"

"Sabrina Morningstar." She extended a hand.

He blinked as he shook it. This was Sabrina? He'd imagined an old, withered widow running this beach-based bed and breakfast.

"I see you found your room." Her smile was positively disarming.

"Yes." He took his hand back and straightened.

Good looks aside, he was here on the job. He was here to debunk the claims that this was a haunted house, and this little stunt she'd just pulled with the door only strengthened his resolve.

He eyed her before inspecting the door, sliding it back and forth. "The door shut on its own."

Her mouth formed a surprised oh, and he instantly disliked the way the fullness of her lips drew his gaze toward them.

"I'm sorry." She began inspecting the base. "I checked with a level to see if there's a slant to the house which might have caused this, but it's even. Then, I replaced the door two months ago. I don't know why this keeps happening."

"I'm not the first?"

"No."

"What about the lock?" he asked.

When she gave him a confused look, he explained, "I was locked outside." He kept his voice firm, perhaps a bit accusatory, as he leveled his gaze at her.

She looked up at him with a quirk of her lips. "I'm afraid that's impossible, Mr. Dalton." She glanced down at the door handle. "There is no lock."

Grant stared at her, a cold prickle climbing his spine.

If there was no lock, then what the hell had trapped him out there?

Two

Sabrina showered, dressed in a simple, pale-green dress, and set to work making dinner—pan seared black sea bass with a Ponchartrain shrimp sauce, roasted potatoes, and broccoli.

Aside from the balcony view, her favorite part of the house was the kitchen with its light oak wood cabinets in a distressed pattern and an island with chopping block and sliding spice racks. She was working on replacing outdated appliances one by one as her bank account allowed.

She seasoned potato wedges with herbs from the garden and roasted them in the oven. Perhaps a good meal would get Grant Dalton's rocky first hour back on track.

He'd looked flustered, with anger sizzling below the surface when she'd opened the door for him. He'd overreacted, or maybe he harbored a fear of being trapped—on an open balcony with a beautiful view. She had no explanation for why his door had stuck, but this old house had more peculiarities than she could fix.

"That smells delicious."

"Oh!" She startled and turned to see her guest standing against the wall between the kitchen and dining room. In her distraction, her forearm bumped the broiling pan as she was transferring it from the oven to the stove.

She hissed as she roughly set down the pan. Guests didn't usually drop into the kitchen before a meal.

"I'm sorry. Are you okay?" Grant moved toward her.

She stuck her arm under the faucet and ran cold water over the quickly reddening surface. "I'm fine."

"No. You're burned. Because of me." He opened the freezer and pulled out an ice cube. "Let me see it."

When she didn't immediately surrender her arm, he took her hand, pulling her arm toward him. He placed the ice cube over the reddened skin.

She barely felt the cold over the warmth of his touch. She stared down at his hand, watching the ice melt against her skin. How long since a man had touched her other than the occasional handshake? Too long.

The contact felt comforting and disconcerting all at once. Certainly, part of the thrill was Grant's attractiveness. He had straight brown hair, combed to one side. Faint sideburns trailed down to a three-day stubble over a strong, defined jaw. He was medium build, medium height, and wore slacks with an off-white, button-down shirt. The sleeves were rolled to his elbows.

No wedding ring.

Yet, he was a guest who'd come here for peace and quiet. She wouldn't ruin his experience by trying to explore the attraction she felt for him.

Finally, she surrendered to the urge to see if he was

enjoying their proximity as much as she was, but when she looked into his face, she saw only a scowl.

Embarrassed and dismayed, she pulled her arm back. "It'll be fine, thank you. If you want to take your seat, I'll have your plate on the table momentarily."

He turned and busied himself uncorking the bottle of pinot grigio she'd set aside for dinner.

"I can get that," she told him. The point of a bed and breakfast was to relax and be waited on.

"I've got it." He poured a glass and carried it to the table in the other room.

She watched him go as something gnawed at the back of her mind. His face and his movements—had she seen Grant somewhere before?

She prepared his plate, poured the Ponchartrain sauce over the fish, and added a sprig of parsley for color. When she carried the plate to the dining room, she found Grant with his back to her as he stared out the window at the ocean view.

She loved that view.

Rather than disturb his tranquil moment, she quietly set down his plate of food and left.

She took her own meal and glass of wine to the balcony for the ocean view. Since the deck extended along the length of the house facing the beach, she went out the kitchen door and sat on the deck furniture off to the end where Grant couldn't see her from the dining room. She didn't want to interfere with his relaxing view. She liked to make her guests feel at ease as if they weren't sharing the space with someone else.

She ate, sipped her wine, and contemplated Thanksgiving with her family.

Could she endure it?

GRANT STARED out the window as the crisp flavor of the wine lingered on his lips. The smell of seasoned seafood and roasted potatoes wafted toward him.

> *The guests are met, the feast is set:*
> *May'st hear the merry din.'*

Was he going to have Coleridge's poem stuck in his head for the rest of his stay here after seeing the painting with the albatross?

Except this was no merry din'. And he wasn't off to a great start—locked out of his room by a door which had no lock. Then, he'd startled Sabrina, and she'd suffered a burn because of it.

And how long had he stood there holding her arm like a moron? Long enough to smell the ocean and citrus scent on her hair. Long enough to envision the bikini top she'd kayaked in earlier. His behavior irritated him, so he'd scowled, which she seemed to have interpreted as directed toward her.

He couldn't possibly be attracted to a woman he hardly knew anything about—his analytical brain forbade impulses. She ran a bed and breakfast at a beach home rumored to be haunted, for crying out loud. They didn't come much more unstable than that.

Still, the warmth from her skin lingered on his fingertips.

The sound of a sliding door from another room brought his attention back to the present. When he turned around, he noticed the plate of food with a wisp of steam coming off the fish. He sat down and took a bite.

Well, she sure could cook. He sloshed wine in his glass. Was she eating right now too? Seemed silly for two adults to be eating the same meal in the same house in two different places. He almost called her name, almost invited her to sit. But he couldn't share a table with someone he might have to publicly humiliate on national TV.

A rush of cool air blew past him, rustling the petals of the lily canberra on the table as a faint the ceiling faintly groaned. He listened but heard no telling noise—no hum of an air conditioning unit, no opening of a window. Where had the breeze originated?

Independent of any other motion, the pale golden liquid in Grant's wine glass rippled. The hair on the back of his neck stood on end.

"Sabrina?"

No answer.

The wine rippled again.

Grant pushed back from the table and stood. She wanted to play games? Fine. He'd catch her in the act.

He started toward the kitchen but caught a glimpse of her radiant blonde hair outside in the garden. She was kneeling in the rich dirt, pulling weeds with a gaze focused only on her task.

If she wasn't behind the strange events in her house,

who was? And was Sabrina ignorant of them or a willing accomplice?

Or were the events the result of something stranger? Something as eerie as the what the Ancient Mariner had witnessed?

> *And some in dreams assurèd were*
> *Of the Spirit that plagued us so;*
> *Nine fathom deep he had followed us*
> *From the land of mist and snow.*

THE NEXT DAY, Sabrina drove to the nearest grocery store where she bought three days' worth of meals. Next, she stopped at *Harold's*—the hodgepodge mom-and-pop corner store had groceries, bait, fresh fish, convenience store amenities, and hardware store products all under one roof.

She picked up new sanding strips and water sealant for the porch. With the weather cooler, she could do more outside work on the house.

"Harold, how are you?" Sabrina set her purchases on the check-out counter.

"Well, hey there." His weathered, brown face crinkled with his smile.

Some of the locals continued to treat Sabrina as an outsider—the city girl who'd bought that old, abandoned beach house—but Harold never had.

"How is your fall garden lookin'?" He rang up her items as he talked.

"Good. Squash is almost ready. I'll bring you some."

She handed him cash. "What's the weather doing this evening?"

He liked to tell people his aching joints predicted rain more accurately than any meteorologist. And darn if he wasn't right most of the time.

"Should be a fine evening for a moonlit stroll on the beach. You got any renters this week?"

"Just one. A writer."

"A man?" He handed her the bag.

"Yeah, a man." She gave him an amused grin.

"You be careful out there alone with a stranger." He shook his head.

"It's okay. I give my guest contact information to my sister, and I have a cell phone and alarm system."

He scratched a few wiry gray hairs on his chin and looked like he wanted to pick her argument apart but decided better of it. "You take care of yourself."

"Always."

Sabrina drove home thinking of Harold's comment. Grant didn't seem threatening, especially the way he'd fussed over her burn. But her guest was guarded. A man with secrets. Well, everyone was entitled to their own pile of secrets.

She had hers—packed into that jewelry sized box. A pang of sorrow struck her gut.

Grant had pre-paid for a week to himself at her bed and breakfast. He could keep those secrets to himself.

GRANT USED the opportunity Sabrina's outing afforded him to plant his cameras. He kept them to communal areas —hallways, kitchen, dining room, and living room. He wasn't here to spy on Sabrina, just the house and anything she may be doing to make it seem haunted. Bedrooms and bathrooms were off limits.

Back in his room, he opened his laptop and fit all six camera images simultaneously visible on his screen to check the angles. So far, so good. And they were all small enough his hostess wouldn't notice.

When his phone rang, he jumped. "Norm, hey. How are you?"

"Grant, what do you have so far?"

"Geez, Norm. I've been here less than twenty-four hours."

His producer could be unbelievably impatient.

"So? Any vibes?"

"Yeah—part vacation retreat, part spooky house. A few strange things, but I haven't found the gimmicks yet. I just got the cameras up."

The expensive gizmos had audio and video *and* automatically transitioned to night vision.

The silence ensuing on the phone was telling, and Grant felt his palms sweat. "It's going to be a good story," he assured Norman. "The owner's a single woman. The house is sixty-years old. Even when I stopped to fill my gas tank and buy snacks, the attendant reported having heard rumors about the house being haunted."

Norman sighed. "I need better than good. Ratings are slipping. I need great. I need an on-camera confession about faking the hauntings."

"Sure, no problem."

Grant ended the call and stared at the six little squares on his laptop screen—the dining room, the hall, the kitchen, the empty foyer.

He pictured Sabrina's face if he forced a confession out of her, imagined those storm-blue eyes red from crying, that bright hair falling over her cheeks. His stomach soured.

If she'd rigged this house to seem haunted, she'd brought the fallout on herself. He told himself that twice.

Then, on the dining-room feed, his untouched wine-glass gave a tiny, solitary ripple.

And no one was in the room at all.

Three

Sabrina stood outside Grant's door holding a tray of food. "Knock. Knock. I brought some snacks. I don't want to bother you. I can leave them outside your door."

Grant opened the door looking haggard in blue jeans and a t-shirt. He stared down at the tray she carried with brows crinkled. He looked exhausted—shadowed eyes, creased shirt. Had she woken him? Or was something else wearing him thin?

"I'm sorry if I woke you."

"No, you didn't. I was just researching."

Was writing so stressful? Perhaps he had personal issues he also wrestled with on this retreat. She tried not to think of Harold's words of caution about her being home alone with a stranger.

"Thank you." He plucked the tray from her grasp—a colorfully arranged mix of meat and cheese with three different beverages—as if it weighed nothing.

"How's your writing going?" She glanced at his laptop on the desk which he'd moved out onto the porch as she'd suggested.

He set the tray down in his room and turned back toward her, the scowl vanished, and his features softened. "Ah. Slow. I haven't been very focused."

"There's a full moon tonight," she began hopefully. "You could take a stroll along the shore. Maybe find some inspiration."

She needed Grant to have a positive experience—maybe leave a nice review of her bed and breakfast or tell a friend. His gaze lightened further, like moonlight itself, as he seemed to genuinely appreciate her suggestion.

No, this man posed no threat to her. He was... he was lonely. Again, her mind tried to identify where she'd seen him before. Years ago, perhaps? But he didn't know her, so she must be imagining the familiarity.

If she asked him, how could that *not* sound like a pick-up line?

'Have we met before?' she asks in a husky voice, followed by awkward silence between them.

Nope. Not happening.

"A moonlit stroll sounds perfect," Grant said.

She backed away from him, stuffing her hands in the back pockets of her blue jean shorts. "Dinner will be ready at six. Blue crab soup. If you come early, please announce your arrival so we can avoid any more self-inflicted injuries."

The corner of his mouth tilted slightly upward. "I'll be sure to thud down the stairs so you know I'm on my way."

"Excellent. See you then." She retreated down the stairs and returned to the kitchen feeling like their interaction had been oddly strained. Probably her fault. She liked looking at Grant's handsome facial features, strong jaw, and smoldering gaze. Next time, she would just leave the snack tray at the door.

LATER THAT EVENING, Grant finished his dinner in the dining room, alone again, and returned to his room to work on his manuscript as the sun set. He propped up in bed on a half dozen mini-pillows as he typed a new scene of his book, incorporating interview notes he'd taken.

People's reported interactions with ghosts were vastly different and seem to vary based on both the medium's ability and the ghost's spiritual strength. There was a mix of auditory and visual encounters—often both but sometimes only one or the other. Age of onset of a person seeing or hearing ghosts was also different. Some only saw a ghost, or ghosts, after an injury or traumatic event. Most ghosts acted helpful in some way to the medium. Rarely did they seem to have any malicious intent. The more research Grant did, the more a recurring pattern emerged: mosts ghosts seemed to have a purpose and often departed from the world of the living when that purpose had been fulfilled.

Part of why he felt driven to do this reality show was because he *did* believe in the paranormal and found it offensive when people tried to pray on believers by creating make-believe haunted places. Most of the show was exposing fakes, but he'd found a few legitimate places where the paranormal dwelled.

When Grant paused to take a break, he stepped out on

the deck under the night sky, careful to put a book in the door to prevent being locked out again. The salt breeze felt instantly refreshing.

He spotted Sabrina as her flashlight danced along the sand. A walk would be nice.

After descending the stairs, he stepped outside onto the lower deck. Using his phone's flashlight, he walked across the wooden bridge and onto the beach.

He wanted to openly announce his arrival because she'd regarded him with strange apprehension at one point as she dropped off his tray. No wonder, he'd realized when he'd looked in the mirror after she'd left. His hair was a mess and his clothes wrinkled. He didn't normally take afternoon catnaps, but the house had been quiet and peaceful as the sound of the ocean drifted through his open balcony door.

And stress bore down on him.

Five years and one hundred episodes later, and his show teetered on the brink of being shut down. The first three seasons had been a smash hit. When their ratings declined during season four, they'd been given one last shot to resurrect their show.

"Good advice about the moon walk," Grant said as Sabrina approached.

"I'm glad you're enjoying it. It's better with the flashlights off. I was using mine to watch the crabs scurry about the sand." She cut off her light.

Grant followed her lead. They turned toward the ocean, and he admired the view—silver crested waves lapping the shore. He glimpsed Sabrina out of the corner of his eye. Soft moonlight haloed her tan skin.

The moving Moon went up the sky,
And no where did abide:
Softly she was going up,
And a star or two beside—

"What are you writing about?" Sabrina asked. "That is, if you're comfortable sharing."

"A book about ghosts."

Her eyes narrowed as her gaze flickered back to the ocean. "You need to work on your pitch."

He elaborated, "The unseen threads that binds us—exploring the supernatural world of ghosts."

"It's a novel?" she asked, brow furrowed slightly in confusion.

"No." He could have lied. He thought about it briefly, making up an alter ego so he could see where a moonlit stroll with Sabrina might lead. But he wasn't the type of man to play make-believe—not for his own motives or to spare someone else discomfort.

"You're really writing about ghosts?"

He tried to gauge her expression. She clearly didn't believe in ghosts.

"Yes. I have a collection of stories from a few mediums who have seen them. Some paranormal detectives, a few physicians, and a museum curator."

"You believe them?"

"I do."

She remained silent a while. He'd obviously made her uncomfortable, but that had been the bitter point—force her in the opposite direction he wanted her to go because if she didn't like him when the truth reared its ugly head, the 'big reveal' of his reality show would be easier.

"Do you believe in ghosts?" he asked.

"I believe in people being haunted by grief or despair or loneliness. Do I think Casper floats around scaring people? No."

"Which of the things you listed is haunting you?"

Something was—evident by her dark gaze and sad smile.

She turned her eyes from the ocean to look at him. "I used to be a nurse. I had fulfillment helping other people."

He waited quietly for her to continue.

"One day, I couldn't help people anymore."

He wanted to know more but didn't press—the same way she hadn't pressed about his belief in ghosts. Some information couldn't be shared in a few days of knowing someone.

She rubbed at her arms. "Anyway, I should get inside and let you enjoy your walk of inspiration."

"Walk with me." The words tumbled out of his mouth, surprising even himself.

"Okay." Her tone echoed more of quiet surrender than eager engagement.

"Tell me about the house. What's it like to run a bed and breakfast?"

They walked down the beach as Sabrina described her beach life. She worked every day on home improvements and admitted not knowing a house could be a full-time job. When she had renters, she explained, she enjoyed ensuring they had a comfortable and relaxing experience.

She asked about his career, and he talked about travel as research for his books, omitting mentioning his haunted house show. Conversation moved to lighter topics— favorites shows, favorite books, favorite foods, favorite pastimes. He was pleased to learn they had more than a few of these overlapping.

When they arrived back at the house, he felt drunk on moonlight and easy conversation with an interesting woman. He bid Sabrina goodnight and took the stairs two at a time to his room.

Spotting his open laptop and the grayscale video feed, his heart sank. He was here to do a job—one likely to destroy Sabrina's peaceful beach getaway home.

His gaze fell on the painting with the albatross over the ship.

> *And I had done a hellish thing,*
> *And it would work 'em woe:*
> *For all averred, I had killed the bird*
> *That made the breeze to blow.*

Feeling like a jerk, he started the shower, stripped, and tried to melt his guilt away under the hot water. After washing, he stepped into the steam-filled room and began to towel off.

A sudden, strange squeaking noise had his pulse racing.

He turned to the source of the noise. In the mirror above the sink, an unseen fingertip drew letters on the moisture-dense surface. His pulse beat rapidly as he stared at the word.

Grant backed up until his shoulders hit the cold tile wall.

This wasn't Sabrina.

And it sure as hell wasn't a trick.

Four

For the next three days, Grant avoided Sabrina. He arrived for meals only after they'd been placed on the table, kept out of the kitchen and main level balcony when he heard her working in these spaces, and waited to go to the beach when she wasn't there.

Spending time in her presence had only further revealed a sweet, enticing disposition. However, drifting into casual, relaxed conversation and exploring the attraction he felt was an indulgence he couldn't afford.

He was under pressure to create a sensational show episode which was likely to infuriate her and shatter any trust they'd been building.

He stared at his laptop and the photo he'd taken of the words on his bathroom mirror.

LEAVE

A chill spread through him, as it had every time he looked at the image. Ironically, the very word would ensure he stayed. This was no trick. He saw the writing of the word as it appeared. He'd tried talking to the spirit every evening since it had delivered its message but received no response. He added a camera to his bathroom, directed only at the mirror.

Three days passed, and no sign of the ghost in his mirror. He had, however, recorded flickering lights in the dining room. He hoped the apparition showed itself. He desperately didn't want to resort to a seance.

His phone rang, and he answered it. "Hi, Norm. How are you?"

"Grant, do you have anything else? I saw the footage you sent me yesterday."

Grant stood and paced the porch. "The footage is intriguing. I think we may be dealing with the real thing here. I was hoping we could take an angle like we did with the Cane Plantation in the third season—sort of a cliffhanger that this could be a truly haunted house."

Norm let out a huff. "I looked at the footage you sent me. Flashing lights? Not real impressive. While the photo of the mirror is creepy, you don't have any video of it happening so the audience will be as unconvinced as I am. We'll need more than this."

"I'm working on it. I still have time."

There was a moment of awkward silence which was quite unusual for Norm. "Just to be clear, you're not avoiding calling this case a fraud because of that Sabrina woman, right?"

"What is that supposed to mean?" A flush spread up Grant's neck.

"I looked at the raw footage. You've got a couple clips of

her walking through the dining room. She's a looker. You'd do good to get her to consent to be on screen."

Grant's jaw tightened. He looked out over the wide spread of ocean. The waves, sloshing and chopping at one another mimicked his own unease.

Sabrina came jogging down the beach, heading toward her kayak just as he'd seen on his first day at the beach house. He enjoyed her company and felt bad for avoiding her.

"Okay. Brutal honesty. She's a pretty woman, and I'm attracted to her. But that doesn't change the fact a ghost is haunting this place. I've found no evidence fraudulent behavior, and I will make a phenomenal story from this paranormal encounter." Attraction was one thing. Compromising the show was another. He wasn't that guy.

"Good. I like the determination I'm hearing. Also, watch the weather radar. There's a tropical storm brewing. Weathermen are bickering over a few different projected trajectories. If it does come close to you, get some dramatic footage of storm clouds and lightning over the beach."

"Yeah, I can do that with the drone."

"I like that. Be careful with the drone if the storm gets too close. That little rascal cost a fair chunk of change."

"It's going to be a great episode, Norm," Grant assured him.

"We're all counting on it."

We.

People's jobs were dependent on him getting more footage on this ghost. The cast consisted of the production crew, editors, and a musician composing the score. Grant needed to discover the spirit's purpose and make it a story worth sharing.

~

SABRINA KNELT IN THE DIRT, ferociously pulling weeds from her garden. Several days had passed since her moonlit stroll with Grant, and he'd been emitting a cool vibe. In fact, he'd been completely avoiding her.

She suspected she knew why. He had seemed familiar to her those first few days of his arrival, but she couldn't place him. Then, the night of their beach walk, when he was spouting about ghosts being real, her memory began to click into place.

At first, she had her doubts, but after their walk, she went to her computer and did an internet search. Her stomach had dropped when his headshot and show logo filled the screen. He was *the* Grant Dalton—star of a reality show about haunted places.

She knew what people said about this place. This was no writing retreat for him. She'd bet the house that his entire presence at her bed and breakfast was a sham. That night, she'd wanted to confront him and throw it all back in his face. Instead, she bottled her emotions and channeled her frustration into housework.

The phone in her pocket buzzed. She retrieved it, smearing dirt on her shorts and phone. "Hello?"

"Hi, Sabrina, just calling to check on you," Lee Ann said.

"I'm fine. Pissed off, but I'm fine."

"What's wrong?"

"My guest writer wanting a beach getaway for inspiration turns out to be none other than the Grant Dalton of the haunted house reality show. No way he's here to work on a book. He's here about the house and the rumors of it being haunted ... rumors I had nothing to do with. He's here to put me on camera and accuse me of inventing reports of ghosts. Like all of the other victims on his show."

"Oh, I know that show. Oh man, some people are made to look really manipulative."

Sabrina stood and brushed the dirt off her knees. "Well, he's the manipulative one."

"What will you do?" her sister asked.

"I want to expose him and tell him to get the hell off my property." Truthfully, part of her wanted to kick him out, and part of her wanted to believe he genuinely liked her. In reality, she'd probably been played. He'd been trying to get her defenses down by talking about some make-believe ghost book he was writing, all the while angling to trip her up so she'd start talking about her house. Maybe he was even recording the entire conversation.

"You could hold it in. Spring his own trap back on him when he tries to expose you. Play his game."

Sabrina considered this as she walked down to the beach to rinse off. Grant had already pre-paid for his stay, and there'd be no getting a good review from him about her bed and breakfast—hence, there were no disadvantages to biding her time and letting things play out against him.

She hadn't concocted a fake haunted house, and Grant Dalton would bury himself in his own deceit.

GRANT LOUNGED on the balcony attached to his room and stared out over the ocean. He hadn't written many words that day. He was distracted thinking about the moonlight stroll with Sabrina.

The woman had an amazing work ethic. She was always in motion—gardening, food preparation, cleaning. He might have been using brain power for his book writing, but he began to feel like a sloth in comparison to her.

Then, there was this ghost issue. A real ghost. Would that be sensational enough if they took the right angle on the show? They could unfold Grant's uncovered pieces of evidence. But without direct visualization of the ghost— which was highly unlikely based on what Grant knew of the paranormal—how sensational could it be? Every story needed a beginning a middle and an end to enthrall viewers.

He needed to know the ghost's purpose.

What's the story here?

So far, he had the photograph of the mirror and a few bizarre pieces of footage from the dining room camera. Not enough.

He needed *great*, according to his producer.

He needed a miracle.

He walked downstairs and followed the sound of a low electric hum and found Sabrina on her hands and knees sanding the porch. Not wanting to say anything and startle her as she wielded an electric power tool, he didn't venture out onto the deck.

Instead, he went to the kitchen where he found her meal plan tacked to the refrigerator. Taco night.

If he couldn't alter the trajectory of his show or his need to unravel the mystery of the ghost, he could at least brown some meat and pretend, for one evening, that they were just two normal people having dinner.

COVERED IN SAWDUST AND SWEAT, Sabrina made her way to the beach. She stripped to her swimsuit and waded into the crisp ocean water. She'd still need to shower, but at least the ocean would wash away a layer of grime. The deck was half sanded now, and she loved seeing the evolution of her work successfully restoring the old house.

When she returned home—towel dried and dressed—the scent of chili powder and Cayenne pepper filled the air. In the kitchen, she found Grant stirring ground beef as it simmered on the stove.

A sudden strange sensation of intimacy struck her at the sight of a man in her kitchen cooking. "What are you doing?"

Grant turned and flashed a disarming smile. "Cooking. I needed to get my nose out of my writing and computer screen and feel useful. I saw your note on the refrigerator—taco night." He wore slacks and his shirt rolled at the sleeves again.

She washed her hands. "Yes, but you're here to relax as a guest, not cook." Her gaze fell to the lettuce, tomatoes, and onions already chopped and ready for the tacos.

Drying her hands, she turned toward the kitchen table, set for two.

"Have dinner with me?" His back was to her as he scooped the seasoned ground beef into a serving dish. "Some company would be nice for a change."

She almost said no. "Okay." She spoke the word hesitantly.

This was an invitation from the man who'd been a recluse the last three days after long lingering gazes on a moonlit beach. What was his new angle? Is this how he would reveal his true purpose? Was this her chance to spring her own trap?

"I'll grab the avocados and cilantro." She reached for the fridge.

"I had to use all of your cilantro."

"For what?" But she saw in the refrigerator a beautiful bowl brimming with chunky guacamole. "Homemade," she said in awe. She pulled it out along with the salsa she'd made earlier and put them on the table.

When all of the taco components adorned the table, Sabrina sat.

"Oh. Almost forgot." Grant retrieved two glasses from the freezer. "Margaritas—on the rocks since I gave up looking for a blender." He stirred the drinks before setting them down on the table.

"I'm amazed you found as much as you did. This looks wonderful." She dipped a chip in the guacamole and her taste buds sprang to life—cilantro, jalapeno, tomato, onion, lime, and salt. She groaned her delight. "Wow."

Grant layered his tacos. "I'm glad you like it."

"It is perfect. It's especially perfect after a day of outdoor manual labor." She used the fresh table ingredients to make a taco salad.

"How are the renovations coming?" he asked.

She swallowed another bite of guacamole, not letting her

guard down. He wanted small talk? She could do small talk. "Good. I power washed the porch and then started sanding. Another day of sanding and I can seal it. Oh, I should have considered the noise. Did the sander disrupt your tranquility?"

"No, no. It's fine. Tell me about the house."

She took a long drink of the margarita before giving him a narrowed gaze. "I was wondering when you were going to ask."

He blinked at her.

"A man writing a book about ghosts doesn't just happen to spend the week at a place rumored to be haunted."

"Busted." He leaned back in his chair.

"Has your time spent here satisfied your curiosity?"

"Your house *is* haunted."

Despite his earnest declaration, she couldn't keep a straight face.

"You're amused," he said.

She arched an eyebrow. "Should I be scared? People have been calling this house haunted even before I moved in here. Apparently, the lady I purchased it from told the locals it was haunted. Then, a few guests commented on strange happenings and even went so far as to post about them on social media. I find this place cozy, not spooky."

"You shouldn't be afraid. Ghosts usually linger to help themselves or help the living. I've rarely heard of anything malicious on their part." He ate his taco.

Half-way through her taco salad, she set her fork down. "What makes you think—after a few days visiting—I have ghosts?"

"Just one, I think. And I've seen activity inexplicable except by paranormal standards."

"I haven't seen anything, and I've been here a year."

"Some people are more receptive to seeing and interacting with ghosts. My abilities are modest at best. But I believe the real reason you don't see any strange activity is because of the necklace you wear."

She reached up and touched the silver pendant. "The previous owner gave this to me. For luck."

"It's a symbol of life and a protective medallion. In ancient Egyptian, the ankh symbolized protection, like the Christian cross. The spirit can't come near you." He drank his margarita.

"You're saying if I stop wearing this, I'd start seeing ghosts?"

"No. But the ghost haunting this place may be able to communicate with you in other ways."

She leaned back as she drank the last of her margarita.

"You don't believe a word I'm saying." When he spoke his words in a wistful tone, she knew he wasn't surprised. He was probably accustomed to people's disbelief.

"You're a grown man, Grant, telling me you see ghosts."

Looking troubled, he moved his plate away and wiped his mouth with a napkin. "I have another confession to make. I am a writer, but I also host a show called *Your Haunted House*. I came here to see if the rumors were true."

"I was wondering if you would tell me what you're up to or just spring the news on me with a camera in my face." Her cheeks grew hot.

He looked stricken. "You knew who I was? All this time?"

"Not at first." She stood and began clearing the table. Irritation flaring through her.

She'd planned to the savor the moment when she exposed him and taught him a lesson in humility. But she felt no victory gloat. She had only warring emotions about a man she wanted to like, his strange belief in the supernatural, and his plan to make a fool of her on his show. She'd watched enough shows to know the outcomes—people's lies exposed on camera with confessions through teary-eyed agony. He'd get none of that from her.

Grant moved around her, clearing the table as she began storing leftovers.

"I should have told you." His voice was low, anguished.

"That's not how the show works though, right? You have to be secretive to catch someone in a lie. Well, now you're caught in your own."

"I never lied."

"True. Deceit, then."

He winced at her hurtful words, though it gave her no satisfaction to shame him.

They moved to washing dishes, working side by side. She tried not to admire how he hadn't slunk away to his room once his identity and intentions were brought to light.

"Why didn't you kick me out when you deduced who I was?" He dried the now clean margarita glasses and shelved them.

"You're a paying customer. Besides, part of me wanted to know what you'd find. I wanted to know what made people think this place was haunted. Of course, I never expected you to tell me it is *actually* haunted. I was hoping for a rational, scientific explanation."

He extended the towel and turned toward her. "I'm sorry, Sabrina. For not being honest with you."

When she took the towel, their hands brushed briefly, sending a jolt of warmth through her. She dried her hands, not making eye contact.

She tried to cling to her anger toward him, but it drained through her like water through her fingers. He had told her the truth, but not at a time or in a way to attempt to publicly humiliate her. His actions held dignity.

"I can honestly tell you that everyone who has been on the show has financially benefited from it. Even the ones caught in lies."

"Has anyone ever sued?" she asked.

He pursed his lips. "Yes. Twice. And we settled."

"I'm not asking because I want to sue. I don't know why I asked. I guess to get a sense of how manipulated people were made to feel."

"I'm sorry."

"And I thought we shared chemistry on the beach." She kept the vulnerability out of her voice. "Perhaps that was my imagination. Or maybe that's just how you get people to let their guard down."

"It wasn't your imagination. And I've never taken a moonlit stroll as a tool of deception." He turned and faced her with a pleading expression. "Forgive me?"

A long moment of silence stretched between them.

"I'm thinking about it." For now, that was the most she could give.

He gave her a boyish grin. "While you're thinking about forgiving me, let me show you something remarkable."

"Show me what?"

"Proof." His gaze flicked toward the stairs. "Of what's really in this house."

"Wait here," Grant said. "I'll bring my laptop down."

"Okay. Mysterious much?" She watched him go, the echo of his footsteps on the stairs.

"You have no idea," he said, voice trailing.

Proof. Of a ghost?

A chill feathered down her spine—half fear, half curiosity.

Five

Grant returned with his laptop and sat beside Sabrina on the couch. She wore shorts and a pink T-shirt over her swimsuit and smelled like salt water from her beach swim and tequila from the margarita.

He'd been part ashamed, part relieved she'd called him out on his dishonesty. After her initial flare of anger, she seemed more curious than upset. She had every right to throw him out of her house, but for some reason she hadn't done so.

He rarely confessed to people that he could sense ghosts. There simply weren't enough people in the world like him or enough proof. He would lose all credibility as a show host. Hosting a debunking show while secretly believing made him feel like a fraud on both sides of the camera.

This probably explained why his book progressed at a snail's pace. How could he reveal real ghost stories to a critical public who'd ridicule and debase him?

40

Tonight, he would see if he could make a believer out of just one person. Start small with one skeptic.

"I'm sorry about the cameras. I installed them in public places only and none of these feeds would be used in the documentary without loads of legal documents and your written permission." He continued despite her reproachful glance and flare of her nostrils, "But the cameras captured something incredible. I've got these little video snippets, recording the overhead light glowing brighter. And it occurs six times each day."

She leaned forward, watching the flicker of light. "What's this one?" She pointed to the single jpg image of the bathroom mirror.

"Ah." He chuckled. "This is a picture of your ghost telling me to leave."

"The ghost left that message for you?" Her eyebrows shot up.

"Wrote it right before my eyes."

"And you didn't run away screaming?"

"I'm not afraid of ghosts. And there's often a reason they're still lingering. Running away screaming benefits no one," Grant said.

"If the ghost has a purpose, why tell you to leave?" she asked.

"Maybe he or she is protecting you."

"From you?" She laughed.

"From strangers putting cameras in your home."

"Hmm. Point taken. I should be thanking it, then." She scowled before her eyes darted back to his screen. "Slow it down. Frame by frame."

He smiled at her enthusiasm, interest, and cleverness.

He moved it frame by frame, pausing at the frame where the glowing light appeared most defined.

He held his breath, waiting to see if she could identify what was hidden there. Coleridge's poem sprang to his mind again.

> *A speck, a mist, a shape, I wist!*
> *And still it neared and neared:*
> *As if it dodged a water-sprite,*
> *It plunged and tacked and veered.*

"It's a symbol," she said.

"Yes. Each flicker captures a symbol." He brought up another image.

"These six today."

She stared for a long moment. "They're numbers, just rotated the wrong way. See? That's a 2 upside down. And that one's a 0, just flipped."

"You're right. If I rotate them correctly in order of when they appeared, we get 011828." He showed her the new image.

"An address? Winning lottery numbers?" she asked.

"Let me line this up with previous days, and then tell me your thoughts."

Sabrina ran a hand through her hair. "And we're sure this isn't just an electrical anomaly?"

He showed her the numbers in rows.

"They're getting smaller." She gasped her realization. "Zero days, eleven hours, twenty-eight minutes," she murmured. "Grant ... it's counting down in real time."

"Exactly. I just figured this out today." He rested a hand on her shoulder.

"A countdown to what?"

"I need to ask the ghost that question."

She made a slight motion to move back from him, but he set down the laptop and took her hands. Soft and warm, but no stranger to manual labor with their small calluses.

"Do this with me, please," he implored. "If nothing happens, you can throw me out and dismiss it as a ruse. If we communicate, then you'll be the first person I've shared all of this with, and maybe you'll believe me as we learn what the ghost thinks will happen when the countdown is finished."

Sabrina's lips quirked. "My negative, skeptical energy isn't going to drive the ghost away?"

"No. That's just fake psychic mumbo jumbo. But I do need you to leave your necklace off for this."

SABRINA SAT across from Grant at the dining room table. She'd removed her necklace per his request and left it on her dresser and felt oddly exposed without it.

He'd arranged candles around the room and incense on the table surface between them. The cinnamon smell wafted through the air.

She might have been unnerved by the idea of summoning a ghost, but Grant appeared adorably flummoxed. He consulted one of his books on how to arrange the candles and incense. His discomfort and absence of any rehearsed motions with the preparations actually set her at ease.

With her permission, he angled his camera to capture the center of the table, excluding a view of Sabrina. She had no desire to make an appearance on any of Grant's footage, legal permission or not.

Grant rubbed his hands together. "Ready?" His voice held an excited, nervous energy.

"You're the captain of this ship. I'm only a spectator." She couldn't help but be amused and entertained by his enthusiasm.

"Spirit of this house," Grant closed his eyes and lifted his hands into the air, "I call upon you to reveal yourself."

Sabrina watched the lazy smoke from the incense drift upward. They sat in silence for a good sixty seconds.

"Is it me?" she asked. "Maybe I'm not a believer, and I'm messing it up." He'd said that couldn't happen, but did he really know?

Grant shook his head. "Spirit, commune with us," he commanded.

After thirty seconds of no response, he dropped his hands to his side. "Well, I feel like an idiot. I've no idea what I'm doing." He sounded more like a boy at his first audition than a jaded host a hundred episodes in.

"If it is any consolation, you looked good doing it."

He gave her a lopsided grin which sent her heart fluttering.

Between them, the incense smoke began to twist unnaturally. It thickened and congregated a foot above the table, behaving more like bloated clouds than smoke. The temperature in the room seemed to drop a few degrees. The gray streams swirled in a circle as wisps tentacled outward, forming the word SABRINA.

After a minute, the cloud-like smoke dissipated, and the incense extinguished.

Sabrina swallowed, feeling a little breathless at having seen her name materialized out of smoke. "That was creepy. I think I'll put my necklace back on now if this is what I've been missing."

Grant rested his hands on the table, staring at the center of the table. "I don't understand. The ghost tells me to leave, then we uncover a countdown, and it finishes with your name. What's the point of lingering as a spirit, if you can't more clearly express yourself?"

"I'm sorry it's frustrating for you."

"I'm more frustrated with myself than anything." He ran a hand through his hair. "I'm not much of a medium."

"Oh, I don't know. I've only known you for less than a week, and already I've seen more paranormal activity from you than during my lifetime before your arrival."

He looked up at her with a pair of grateful brown eyes.

She turned away and stood. "But I don't know what to make of cryptic messages, and it's late." She was too wound to be tired.

All the talk of paranormal activity had her head spinning. And the more time she spent with Grant, the more she liked him. She couldn't let herself become too attached to a man who'd be moving on soon to the next haunted house.

"I'll see you in the morning," she said.

Grant remained seated at the table. A droop of disappointment tugging the corners of his mouth created a slight pouty dejection, like a teenager denied the keys to borrow the car.

Sabrina kept her smile to herself and patted his shoulder in a measure of comfort before going upstairs.

GRANT WOKE WITH A START, sitting up in bed. He listened, trying to figure out what had dragged him from sleep. He slung off the covers, intending to check the bathroom since that was the only place in his room the ghost had previously revealed itself.

"Grant?" A tentative woman's voice at his door.

"Sabrina?" In three quick strides, he arrived at the door and pulled it open.

"Are you okay?" she asked. She wore pink cotton pajamas, revealing bare legs and arms.

Grant was reminded of the first day he saw her—white swimsuit against tan skin.

He cleared his throat. "I was going to ask you the same thing."

She glanced around him into his room. "I thought I heard noises." She chuckled nervously. "I'm probably hearing things or overreacting to the normal squeaks and moans of this old house." She wrapped her arms around herself. "All this ghost talk. I guess I'm having trouble sleeping."

"Me too. Every time I close my eyes, I see the countdown—glowing letters in swirling smoke. How about this?" He opened the door wider, walked to the bed, and smoothed the comforter over the top. "We'll watch a show on my laptop as a distraction." He piled the pillows against the headboard. "And with a thousand decorative pillows, it will feel like we're on a sofa." He began moving the pillows he'd stacked in one corner back onto the bed.

He wouldn't normally invite a potential show guest into his room, but there was nothing normal about this house or his interaction with its owner.

She stepped tentatively into the room.

"I'm open to other suggestions," he said, "but you don't have a living room set up to watch shows. And this spot is more comfortable than the couch downstairs."

"You don't like my pillows?"

"I like your pillows. I've just never slept in a bed where the pillows occupied more space than I do."

She sat and leaned back on the mound of pillows. "What are we watching?"

"How about anything but ghost stories or horror?" He brought his laptop over and placed it between them on the bed to let her know his intentions were purely platonic.

He'd crossed enough lines by invading her home with his cameras, summoning ghosts in her dining room, and stealing small moments of physical contact with her. Anything more was unconscionable.

She crossed her legs as she scrunched her face in contemplation. "Something with action."

"The world needs saving and only one man can do it?"

She smiled. "Yes. Or one woman."

"Hmm. How about *Tomb Raider*?"

"Yes! Tomb Raider. Good idea."

He logged into his computer and found the movie online. To his relief, the ghost didn't make another appearance that night. Grant's cameras still filmed the light flickering in the dining room downstairs, but he would follow up on those recordings tomorrow. For now, he enjoyed the show and the proximity to Sabrina.

He noticed she'd put the necklace back on.

~

HALF-WAY THROUGH THE MOVIE, Sabrina and Grant laughed at themselves for picking a show with a count-down to catastrophic doom.

They turned off the movie, and Grant closed his laptop.

It was after midnight, and Sabrina knew she should go back to her own room. Yet, something of Grant's transition tonight to friendly behavior had her wanting to linger longer.

She ran a finger over the healing burn on her forearm, remembering what his initial touch had felt like—gentle yet strong, simultaneously grounding her and carrying her into the lightness of floating, as if on glassy, tranquil sea water.

Grant copied her, touching a tender finger to her skin. "I still feel bad about that."

Before she could speak, his finger trailed down to her hand where his hand settled gently.

"Why do you isolate yourself out here? Why did you leave nursing?" he asked.

She stiffened, but he kept hold of her hand, stroking it lazily with his thumb in soothing motions. She wondered if he'd looked her up on the internet after she told him she was a nurse. She couldn't fault him. She'd done the same when she'd realized who he was, only to discover he was quite the celebrity in some circles.

What would her confession to a stranger matter? He

could judge her and leave. Was he a stranger? They'd shared a meal, he'd watched her name appear in smoke, and held her hand in a séance. Talking with him would buy her a little more time by his side—an unfamiliar place which surprisingly offered security and peace of mind.

"I caused the death of a patient." She paused, anticipating repulsion from him, but he didn't shrink back from her. "He was seventeen and had cystic fibrosis. I had orders to treat his breathing exacerbations with nebulizers and an antibiotic. I did the usual pre-administration checks—right drug, right patient. And I asked about allergies first. Then, I hooked up the antibiotic to his IV and set up the pump."

She sniffed. "He sat straight up in bed—eyes wide and face flushing. I'll never forget that look. 'Something's not right,' he said. 'You're okay', I told him." She scoffed. "*You're okay*. The single worst lie of my entire life. He had an anaphylactic reaction to the antibiotic. His airway closed and blood pressure plummeted. The ER physician couldn't resuscitate him." She still remembered the smell of alcohol swabs, the squeak of the wheel on the crash cart as it was brought to the bedside, and the boys bare chest during compressions.

"He reacted to the antibiotic?"

"Yes. He had a penicillin allergy. Ten percent of people with a penicillin allergy have cross-reactivity with the class of antibiotic I gave my patient. I should have known of the interaction from my nursing pharmacology training."

"But you had no way of knowing if he'd be in the ten percent. This is a tragedy, Sabrina, not negligence on your part."

"That's what the morbidity and mortality review board

decided. But I'm the one who watched him die. I'm the one who pressed START on the IV pump."

"You've been blaming yourself for how long now?" Grant asked.

"Over a year."

He pulled her to him.

Having deprived herself of affection and understanding since the event, she didn't resist. "The medication I administered took his life. *I* took his life." She choked on the words as she lay her head against his chest.

"His death is not your fault, Sabrina. It's not your fault."

She stayed in his arms, allowing herself to be soothed— like eucalyptus over a raw throat. She fell asleep to the sound of Grant's steady beating heart and feel of his hand stroking her hair.

But somewhere in this old house, the countdown was still running.

Six

rant woke to the smell of ocean spray and tropical, feminine skin lotion. He blinked his eyes open to light from the gray sky outside his window. Beside him, curled in the covers while he'd slept above them, lay Sabrina with short, tousled blonde hair.

It took surprising effort to not pull her into his arms. Intending to spare her an awkward morning after an intimate, though non-sexual night, he grabbed clothes and his phone and went to take a shower.

After washing, he stepped out into the steamy room, tentatively checking the mirror for signs of the ghost.

Nothing.

He dried and wrapped the towel around his waist as a thought occurred to him.

"Spirit, are you with me?" he whispered.

YES, the words appeared in the mirror.

Goosebumps spread along his arms. "Are you the patient who died in front of Sabrina?"

A moment passed as the window steamed back over the previous words and another *YES* appeared.

Grant fumbled with his phone laying on the countertop, setting it to record and angling it at the mirror. He'd forgotten to turn on the laptop camera to record.

"What's your name?"

PATRICK

"Do you have a message for Sabrina?"

FORGIVENESS

A lump formed in Grant's throat. Forgiveness. The one thing Sabrina couldn't give herself.

"And what is the countdown?" Grant asked. "Are you trying to warn us about something?"

Heart racing, Grant stopped recording on his phone and opened his weather app.

Oh, crap. If the storm continued toward them, timeline to landfall matched Patrick's countdown.

Two minutes later, Grant stepped out of his bathroom to an empty bedroom. He rushed to dress in khaki pants and a button-down shirt.

"Sabrina?" he called, rolling his sleeves.

No answer.

He ran a brush through his hair before leaving the bedroom and bounding down the stairs.

"Sabrina?"

All the lights were off. He searched the living room, the dining room, and the deck. Maybe she'd taken a walk on the beach.

In the kitchen, Grant found a note.

Picking up eggs for breakfast.
~Sabrina

On the counter, coffee brewed in the machine. He poured a cup and stepped out on the deck. The choppy waves beneath a gray sky mimicked his own unsettled stomach—small signs of the devastation to come.

FEELING LIGHTER THAN AIR, Sabrina parked at Harold's and entered the store. She smoothed down her blue dress and grabbed a cart.

The entire drive she'd kept telling herself not to read too much into her night with Grant. But conversation had flowed effortlessly, and he'd been the one to offer a comforting touch.

She felt as though a weight had been lifted, confessing her guilt and sorrow over Patrick's death. She hadn't known how much she needed to open up about the tragic event.

Then she'd spent blissful hours sleeping in Grants arms. But not waking up in them. Probably better that way. What would she have said? Thanks? Or sorry? She had, after all, grieved on his shoulder and then stolen his blankets.

She loaded eggs, cheese, green peppers, onions, and mushrooms into her cart. She decided to cook him breakfast, have a normal conversation over omelets, and let him broach the topic of their chemistry or the possibility of a future relationship.

"Mornin', Miss Sabrina."

"Morning, Harold."

He began to ring up her groceries. In a corner behind the counter, his granddaughter played with action figures. She wore pink overalls, and her hair was woven in braids. Sabrina had seen Gina entertaining herself in the store on several occasions. She had never asked about the girl's parents, but she had the impression Harold mostly cared for her.

"No milk and bread? These old bones promise it'll be a doozy."

"Doozy?" Sabrina followed Harold's gaze toward the mounted television screen.

HURRICANE PIKE

Bold letters at the bottom of the screen were overshadowed by gray swirling clouds off the South Carolina Coast. The hair on her neck stood on end—swirling clouds like the smoke from the incense. The last time she'd checked the weather, it had been a distant tropical storm over the ocean.

The ghost had been trying to tell them about the storm! This was the countdown.

Ice cold needles pricked along her spine and sent a

throbbing sensation along her temples, like brain freeze from drinking a slushy too fast.

"Weatherman's sayin' it won't make landfall," Harold said. "It's gonna turn back out to sea, but we'll get some wind and waves. Plenty of rain, too."

He told her the total, and she paid for her groceries.

She didn't believe the forecast. The ghost had gone through the trouble of trying to warn them about the storm and wouldn't do that if this wasn't its destination. "It's going to hit us, Harold. You and Gina should get away from the coast--now."

"Well, now. This store has survived more than a few storms. We'll be fine."

If not for the ghost, she might have shared the same opinion about her house. Instead, she needed to get back to Grant so they could evacuate.

GRANT PACED the house as entirely too much information swirled through his mind about hurricanes. Having never been in proximity to one, he'd done an internet search about hurricanes this century. Matthew, Felix, Dean, Irma, Wilma, Maria, Rita, and Katrina were a few of the deadliest. Some of them reached wind speeds up to one hundred eighty miles per hour. Images of Sabrina's house blown into the Atlantic Ocean flowed through his imagination.

They needed to evacuate.

When he heard the engine of Sabrina's car, he walked out of the house and down the stairs to see her. She gave him a weak smile, but she looked pale—like she'd seen a gh—.

Hmm. He needed a different analogy.

She opened the door to the back seat and reached for her groceries. He stopped her with a touch and spun her into his arms. She returned the embrace, and her proximity eased an ache in his chest. He'd worked himself into worry waiting for her.

"What was that for?" She leaned back far enough to look into his eyes.

"I needed a hug."

She must have as well, because already her color looked better. When she smiled, his heart swelled. How easy would it be to lean down and offer a kiss? He almost did, but a gust of wind reminded him of looming danger.

Sabrina spoke first, "I know what the ghost is warning us about. There's a hurricane."

With pursed lips, Grant nodded and released her. He reached around her and picked up the grocery bags.

"How did you know?" she asked.

"Pat—" he stumbled over the word, not wanting to reveal the identity of the ghost yet and cause Sabrina's wounds to reopen. They needed to discuss the storm first. "After my shower, I had another message in the mirror. This one said *storm*."

Hands full, they climbed the stairs and walked to the kitchen.

Grant set the groceries on the counter. "I checked the dining room video, and the ghost left another number. We have four hours before the hurricane hits."

"Meteorologists are in disagreement over the trajectory.

Some say it won't hit land," she said in a tone suggesting she didn't believe the news.

"Your ghost disagrees. And I bet the weather reporters will be changing their tune soon. I'm packed. You should, too."

"I have to get this place boarded up, but you should go." She avoided eye contact as she put away groceries.

"I'll help. The storm prep will go faster with two people. I've never hurricane-proofed a house before, so you'll have to tell me what to do."

She grinned before arching a seductive eyebrow. "I've never had a man give me free license to tell him what to do."

"For today, in the interest of facilitating an evacuation, you may instruct me on how best to help."

"Ah, well. Now you've added all these parameters and stipulations, it won't be as much fun." She put away the rest of the groceries.

He liked her flirting but would enjoy it more when the threat of a hurricane wasn't looming over them. "I promise fun when we're out of the storm's reach."

FOR THE NEXT HOUR, Sabrina and Grant worked to secure the house. They locked all the beach lounge chairs in the storage room in the basement and brought the kayak and oars indoors from the outdoor rack beneath the house.

Grant closed the windows and secured the shutters while Sabrina bolted the doors. She felt glad she'd already checked the roof last month—replacing curled shingles, covering bald spots, and sealing seams.

The deck posed a risk, she knew. The upper deck had a

few old boards and posts. A person could lounge there, but it might not survive hundred mile-per-hour winds.

She packed clothes and brought her suitcase to the front door. "I think she's as protected as she can be." She patted the nearest beam of the house, still worried about the upper windows and the deck she'd been repairing.

Grant sat at the dining room table looking grim.

"What's wrong?" she asked.

He turned his laptop toward her. "There are accidents and fender benders blocking every highway."

She looked at the interactive map on the screen where all westbound roads glowed red. "There must have been a mass exodus attempt when the media announced the hurricane turned toward land."

As she sank into the chair opposite him, guilt settled into her stomach. She'd just doomed them to waiting out a hurricane in beach front property. "I'm sorry, Grant, if we'd left when you said to leave, we might not be stuck here."

"It's not your fault." He gave her a weak smile.

"How about that breakfast?" He pushed up from the chair. "I'll cook."

She realized they hadn't eaten yet today. Cooking a warm meal while they still had power seemed like a good idea.

"I'll go check the generator and set up candles."

When Sabrina passed through the house, she checked her phone and noticed a missed call. She picked up her mobile phone from the kitchen counter and called her sister back.

"Hi, Lee Ann."

"Sabrina, are you okay? Are you evacuating?"

"I'm fine. I can't evacuate—the mass exodus jammed the roads. I've storm-proofed the house as best I can. I have food, water, and a generator."

"Oh, Sabrina." Her voice was all anguish. "Your house is *on* the beach. We're all worried sick."

"Projections don't have a direct hit on this part of the North Carolina coast."

"But your house is so old. And you're all alone."

"An old house means it has survived plenty of storms." —Or that it limped along on its last leg until a stiff wind pummeled it. Sabrina wondered how she was able to speak so calmly when her insides felt as knotted as the worry in Lee Ann's voice. "Besides, I'm not alone."

"The renter is still there?"

"Yeah, he's helping me. He's actually a nice guy and apologized for not being honest from the beginning."

"This is the ghost fraud exposer you told me about? I watched a few episodes of his show. He's good looking!"

"Ah. Yes, he is."

"In one episode, he rushed out of his room in the dead of night with only blue jeans on and the camera caught him just as he was pulling on his shirt."

Huh. Sabrina hadn't seen that episode.

"Look. I need to get back to work." She ran a hand through her short hair. "Cell towers might go down, but I'll call you when this is over."

"Be safe." Lee Ann's voice turned high-pitched, as though holding back tears or hysteria—or both.

"Hey, Lee Ann."

"Yeah?" She sniffed.

"I'll see you at Thanksgiving."

If I survive this, I'm done hiding.

∼

AROUND THE TIME the one-hundred-mile-per-hour winds arrived, the power went out. Grant sat on the couch with Sabrina curled into him. Around them, the house shuddered and moaned. They kept away from windows even though they were boarded, and this room had the strongest support beams.

Candles on the table flickered soft light. Since they wouldn't know how long the power would be out from wind and flooding, they planned to wait to start the generator.

> *And the coming wind did roar more loud,*
> *And the sails did sigh like sedge,*
> *And the rain poured down from one black*
>   *cloud;*
> *The Moon was at its edge.*

Grant had never experienced a hurricane. Wind and rain pounded mercilessly against the house. The wood creaked and moaned as if it would succumb to the storm at any moment and be whisked away. He was reminded of the house from the *Wizard of Oz* even though this was a hurricane rather than a tornado.

> *And now the STORM-BLAST came, and he*

61

Was tyrannous and strong:
He struck with his o'ertaking wings,
And chased us south along.

Grant threaded his fingers into Sabrina's and searched for words of reassurance. "A friend of mine films tornados. He's probably shot over a hundred storms and is still alive to keep filming more."

He traced a finger from his other hand along her clavicle. "You took off the necklace."

Sabrina shrugged. "I packed it. I figured if the ghost had something else important to tell you, I shouldn't block its message."

"I have something I want to show you. This is from this morning." He pulled out his phone and replayed the video of the bathroom mirror, bracing himself for her anger—either because she thought he fabricated the video or because he hadn't shown it to her sooner.

Instead, her face lit with surprise. "Oh. It's been Patrick this whole time?"

"I was afraid you'd think I made this up."

"How could you have? Even if you had some wicked photo editing skills, I never told you his name. And no social media or internet search would have revealed it to you." She leaned back against Grant as she dabbed a tear away from her eye. "Nice of him to look out for me, except that if you hadn't shown up, I'd never have known he's been haunting me."

"Glad I could help." He ran a hand up and down her arm in a soothing gesture.

"But, the stories of house hauntings predated my arrival here."

Grant nodded. "I contemplated that. You said the previous owner gave you that necklace for luck. I bet she had a ghost. Maybe she assumed the ghost would remain after she left, and gave you the ankh to keep it away."

"So, her ghost might still be haunting her. Are certain places ghost magnets?"

"Ghosts can be linked to objects, places, or people. In Patrick's case, he probably followed you here."

"All of this to warn me. To protect me." She took his hand and threaded her fingers through his. "I'm so thankful you came, Grant."

When she looked up at him, her lips were tantalizingly close to his. His heart thudded faster as he leaned closer, agonizingly slow to give her time to reject him before his lips touched hers.

Instead, she arched up and kissed him. In the softness of her mouth, he forgot about ghosts and the relentless pounding of rain and wind against the side of the house. The swirling gusts of the hurricane were lost to his ecstasy as he drowned himself in the passion of their kisses.

Somewhere beneath them, the house groaned as another gust slammed into its sides.

Seven

Sabrina woke to utter stillness.

Her night had been spent embracing Grant, listening to the storm clawing relentlessly at the house, and waiting to see if Hurricane Pike would rip the walls to shreds and carry them into the ocean.

She wondered if most people along the coast had managed to safely evacuate.

Now, the world outside sounded as calm as the man sleeping beside her. Although she was tempted to remain close to this amazing man—producer, medium, empathetic listener, phenomenal kisser, and maker of a mean omelet—she wanted to see the damage to the house.

She crept out of bed, still dressed in jeans and a t-shirt, and padded downstairs. The sight out of the sliding glass door stole her breath. Water surrounded the house, as if they'd been swallowed by the ocean, and the porch was ... gone. The stilts creaked, and she was grateful they'd held. She shuddered and gaped at so much water, wondering how long it would take to recede. Would her car even function or had it been flooded—or washed away?

How long might they be trapped here?

Generator time.

She turned it on and started coffee brewing. As the aroma filled the house, she looked back out the window.

GRANT WOKE to an empty bed but an intact house. He heard Sabrina's footsteps downstairs as he rolled out of bed and stretched. Walking to the window, he slid it up and he moved the shutter from view.

He pulled another piece of equipment out of his travel bag and powered on the drone and remote control. He'd thought about flying it before the storm to film pre- and post-hurricane footage—if he survived—but by the time he'd helped Sabrina take measures to protect the house, the winds were too strong.

As he directed the drone out the door and flew it over the coast, he watched the live feed on his laptop. Land and roads were covered in stagnant, brown water. The tops of houses and trees gave the only indication of where the ocean border should be. The top half of cars were visible in most places, so he estimated the water was only a few feet deep. A child's bike floated past a house with a missing roof.

> *I looked upon the rotting sea,*
> *And drew my eyes away;*
> *I looked upon the rotting deck,*
> *And there the dead men lay.*

Nothing seemed to stir. With a sinking feeling, Grant wondered how many people had been stranded by the hurricane and how many houses had drifted away in the torrent and were no longer there.

~

ARMS WRAPPED around Sabrina from behind. "I'm sorry about your house." Grant's tender embrace warmed her.

"It's still standing." She wasn't upset about the loss of her deck. "We survived. The rest is just rebuilding."

He kissed her neck. "Is this okay? You'll let me know if I'm too much? I like being close to you—with or without a deadly storm."

"I like you, too." She turned in his arms, intending to elaborate on that when his words caught her attention. "Was it deadly?"

Grant reached for his laptop on the kitchen table and attempted to log in. "Internet's down. Let me see if I can use my phone as a hot spot." He synchronized the two.

Together, they scanned the media reports. Yes, the storm had been deadly. Thousands were without power, and hundreds were stranded due to flooding and debris.

Sabrina took a moment to send a text to Lee Ann from her phone to let her know she was okay.

Grant's computer screen flickered.

"What was that?" Sabrina asked. "You're not connected to a power source, so why the surge?"

"Patrick," Grant said. "I can feel him." He moved quickly over to the coffee table in the living room where several candles sat. He lit three and pushed them together. The flames glowed, and their smoke streams merged.

When smoke tentacled up from each candle, she sucked in a breath. The streams mingled. She wrung her hands together as she waited. What would Patrick's message be? Good news or another countdowns?

The smoke formed letters:

HELP HAROLD

"Harold?" Sabrina's mouth went dry. She took a step closer to the flames, but Grant held up his hand for her to stay back. Sudden motion would create air movement and disrupt the smoke.

"Who's Harold?" he asked her.

"He's the sweet old man who runs the grocery store. He has a granddaughter who, I think, lives with him."

Grant turned back toward the candles' flames. "Patrick, are they in danger now? Do we need to help them now?"

NOW

Sabrina set her jaw. "Give me five minutes to change and grab my first aid kit." She had an advanced kit she'd put together from her medical knowledge—more diagnostic tools than commercial first aid kits though still limited in what she could treat. She carried over-the-counter remedies only.

"I'll see if I get one of our cars running... if we still have cars."

Sabrina pulled on her wet suit and water shoes. She

doubted she'd be swimming, but wading was likely, and the suit would keep her dry and warm.

Her first aid kit wasn't waterproof, so she dropped it and her phone in a gallon plastic bag and sealed it shut.

Harold.

Worry crawled along her skin and settled with unease into her stomach. She thought about the elevation of his store and recalled it being only slightly higher than the road around it. Had it flooded, too?

The front door of her house swung open. Grant entered, pants soaked up to his thighs. "Both cars are flooded."

Sabrina glanced at the kayak against one wall in the entry room. "I have an alternative means of transport."

Grant glanced at the kayak and back at Sabrina. He set his jaw. "There's going to be debris and power lines. I'm not letting you go alone."

"Okay. I'll take any help I can get."

GRANT CARRIED the boat down the porch steps and set it in the high water. The flooding had crept up over the tires of Sabrina's car. He glanced disparagingly at his own car which appeared to have been slung at an angle down to the street curb.

The kayak rocked, and cold water sloshed around them as they took turns climbing into it—Grant in front and Sabrina in back. The water chilled his skin; he didn't have a wetsuit like Sabrina. She stuffed her first aid kit and flashlight bags under her seat.

They paddled in unison with Sabrina also steering.

Houses stood in varying degrees of disarray. They were all flooded, but some had been built high enough on stilts, like Sabrina's, where the interior wouldn't be wet. Others were partially underwater. Power lines hung like limp noodles—down, but also dead. Shingles and decks had abandoned their houses. Homes were peppered with shattered windows and displaced shutters.

Around them, debris floated—wood from dismantled decks and sheets of corrugated metal ripped from people's sheds and carports. They maneuvered slowly around the hazards, hoping not to snag on anything lurking beneath the muddy, greenish-brown water. When they bumped something submerged, they nearly tipped.

The post-hurricane scene was so eerie and desolate, it seemed almost post-apocalyptic.

Grant broke the silence:

> *"Day after day, day after day,*
> *We stuck, nor breath nor motion;*
> *As idle as a painted ship*
> *Upon a painted ocean.*
>
> *Water, water, every where,*
> *And all the boards did shrink;*
> *Water, water, every where,*
> *Nor any drop to drink."*

"I've heard that poem before. Where is that from?" Sabrina asked.

"Coleridge's *The Rime of the Ancient Mariner*. I saw a great blue heron fly over us just now and thought of the albatross in the poem. Actually, the poem has been in my head since I saw the albatross in the guest room of your house. It's about a ship stranded after a storm."

"Hold up a minute." She lifted her oar out of the water and looked over the landscape of brown and gray. "I'm losing my bearings here."

Grant turned around and grinned. "It's not like we can stop and asked for directions."

"Would you stop and ask directions?" she teased.

"I am not above asking directions. I'll prove it to you." He straightened and cleared his throat. "Patrick, can you give us some guidance to Harold's store?"

"Patrick is with us now?"

He shrugged. "I don't know. We'll find out."

They scanned the water and scenery around them, looking for a sign. A shadow passed overhead, and Grant looked up to the sky.

"Would you look at that?" he marveled.

In the sky, soared a great, white albatross.

"What is it?"

"An albatross. They're Southern hemisphere birds. It shouldn't even be here."

The bird circled above them as it descended before taking a trajectory north.

"Wow," Sabrina said. "Let's follow that bird."

SABRINA'S PALMS felt raw from paddling by the time they arrived in the parking lot of Harold's store. His sign dangled on a slant, barely holding on by a few nails on one side. Half of the roof had vanished. They climbed out of the boat and tied it off to ensure it wouldn't float away.

Once inside, they trudged through the water inside the store. The building was elevated enough that only a half foot of stagnant, muddy water filled the grocery aisles.

"Harold?" Sabrina called. "Are you in here?"

Barely, over the sound of tiny sloshing waves from their wading, she heard a small whimpering.

They followed the noise toward the back of the store, struggling over and around pieces of the roof and fallen, soggy insulation. They arrived at a closed wooden door.

Sabrina turned the handle and pushed. The door didn't budge.

"It's stuck," she said, throwing her weight against it to no avail. She stopped, panting. "It's not locked, but it won't open."

"We passed hatchets in the outdoor section of the shop," Grant said. "I'll be right back." He vanished around the corner.

"Gina, honey. It's Sabrina." She spoke into the door. "I'm a friend of your granddad. I need to chop down the door. It will be loud. I need you to stay away from the door." She listened but heard no more whimpering. She would take that as a good sign.

Grant returned, peeling the protective wrapper off the hatchet. "Step back."

She gave him room to work. In five swift strikes, he had a hole large enough to peek through.

He peered inside. "Looks like he tried to stem the flooding into the room with bags of soil and rice. I'll have to make a hole big enough to climb through." He inspected the door frame, then hacked a horizontal line just above the door handle.

Using the butt of the hatchet, he opened the top half of the door. It swung out of the way, into the room, still attached by the top hinge. He climbed over it before helping Sabrina avoid the jagged wood.

"Thanks."

The room was a back office. The small girl sat on a desk clutching her knees and pulling them up into her chest. Her face was puffy from crying.

"Gina?" Sabrina said softly. "Do you remember me? I'm one of Harold's customers. This is Grant. And we're here to help."

Harold was slumped over the desk in an office chair.

"You check on him, I'll take care of Gina," Grant said.

Sabrina pushed her legs through the half foot of water and reached for Harold. She felt for a pulse—present and strong, but his skin felt clammy.

On the off chance he was in a heavy slumber—unlikely through Grant's hacking—she gently shook the shop owner. "Harold? Can you hear me?"

No response.

She tugged at his medical alert bracelet and twisted so she could read it.

DIABETES

Insulin dependent or not?

She ran her fingers over the tips of his digits, feeling for calloused skin from lancet pricks. There, on the side of his ring finger, she found the bumps. Since he was routinely checking his blood sugar with finger sticks, he was likely insulin dependent rather than only on oral hypoglycemic medications.

Next question: pump or self-injection?

"Gina, do you ever see your granddad injecting medication into his skin? Giving himself shots for his sugar diabetes?"

The sullen girl nodded without speaking, but her eyes darted to the right. Sabrina followed her gaze and noted a small refrigerator in one corner.

"Grant, can you check the fridge for insulin?"

Sabrina opened her first aid kit and pulled out her glucometer. She needed to know if his blood sugar was too high or too low.

As she pricked his finger and ran the test, Grant set the vial of insulin and a syringe on the desk. He talked in a soothing voice to Gina about how Sabrina was helping her granddad.

Sabrina stared at the digital read out—whatever Harold's blood sugar was, it was too high for her instrument to read, which meant it peaked over five or six hundred; she couldn't recall exactly from the package insert the maximum level the machine could detect.

"How bad?" Grant asked.

Way above what her meter could read. Her stomach dropped—but her hands stayed steady.

"Hyperglycemia," she said. "He needs an emergency room, IV fluids, and an insulin drip."

"How did his blood sugar get so high with his insulin right here with him?"

"If I had to speculate, he probably wasn't checking his levels regularly as he dealt with the storm and flooding. Add to that drinking juice—" she gestured to empty bottles lying around "--instead of water, his blood sugar would climb. Between the fatigue of sleep deprivation, exhaustion from barricading the place, and acidosis caused by high blood sugar, he probably wasn't thinking clearly. Maybe just thought he'd just lay his head down to rest for a minute and then didn't wake up."

"I'll see if I can get through to emergency services. Can you help him?" Grant asked.

She started to draw up Harold's insulin and counted how many test strips she had. Eleven left. "I can help him." She could bring his blood sugar down with his own short-acting insulin. "But I will eventually run out of either insulin or test strips, so I need an ETA from EMS."

GRANT TRIED to be helpful as Sabrina worked tirelessly, checking Harold's blood sugar every hour and giving insulin injections. When the man became semi-lucid, he said something about his car not starting for him to be able to evacuate before the storm struck.

Grant focused on making friends with Gina in hopes the experience would overall be less traumatizing. He piggy-backed her through the store to find water and snacks, acting as though he couldn't navigate without her. By the end of their grocery gathering, he'd helped her relax and perhaps forget her fear at the situation of her grandfather's illness and strangers in his wrecked store.

Six hours passed before the water receded enough for an ambulance to arrive.

Grant stood by as Sabrina told the paramedics what she'd done to treat Harold's elevated blood sugar. She'd written down everything for them—dosing in units and time administered.

When she finished, she came beside Grant and wrapped an arm around him. Together they watched the ambulance doors close as Harold gave them a wave with his granddaughter seat-belted in beside his stretcher.

Grant squeezed his arm around Sabrina and kissed her cheek. "You were amazing."

"Thanks. It felt good to save a life."

"He's going to be okay?"

"Yes. Probably just a day or two in the hospital fixing his sugar and electrolytes. We should thank Patrick."

"He usually makes an appearance after a hot shower or by candle smoke." He pressed his lips briefly to the side of her forehead.

She leaned against him. "Hmm. A hot shower by candlelight sounds wonderful."

As they turned back toward the ruined streets and the waiting kayak they'd have to carry back, Sabrina glanced up at the washed-out sky.

For the first time in a long time, the guilt in her chest eased.

Somewhere, she hoped, Patrick was finally at peace.

Eight

6 MONTHS LATER

Grant lounged in the chair beside Sabrina, watching the golden sun rise over a gentle ocean on the brand new deck. He still thought of bits of the poem whenever they were back at the beach house, but the memories were pleasant.

> *The Sun came up upon the left,*
> *Out of the sea came he!*
> *And he shone bright, and on the right*
> *Went down into the sea.*

He glanced at the woman who wore his favorite white swimsuit and shorts, like the first time he'd seen her on the beach.

Sabrina had reentered the workforce as a nurse, doing

locum tenens assignments—the kind of short-term contracts that let her follow Grant wherever his next haunted site took him.

Sabrina's story had saved Grant's ghost show. The audience loved the idea a silent spirit had saved lives. Grant convinced his producer to keep everyone involved anonymous. The success of the episode thrilled him, but he would be perfectly satisfied to never weather another hurricane in a beach house.

Patrick moved on. One candlelit dinner after Sabrina had started working again, he simply said GOODBYE— letters in a stream of smoke that dissolved away the last of her guilt.

After his farewell, Sabrina began wearing the necklace again. She'd said she appreciated Grant's gift but would prefer him to be the only one to interact with spirits.

Looking out over the ocean, he reached over and took her hand. "I'm so thankful I came to your haunted house."

"I'm glad Patrick's presence brought you here. And I appreciate you pulling me out of isolation."

He kissed the hand he held. "You would have gotten there eventually. Helping people is part of who you are, but I don't mind being part of you rediscovering your passion."

"That's not the only passion I've rediscovered."

"I don't mind being a part of that either."

"You, me, and a romantic stroll on the beach?" she offered.

"I'll be there."

For the first time in over a year, Sabrina could look at the sunrise and think of beginnings rather than endings.

<<<***>>>

***** QUICK NOTE FROM THE AUTHOR *****

READY FOR ANOTHER sweet and magical romantic suspense? There are so many delights to enjoy! Keep scrolling for the first chapter in the next book.

Romancing the Spirit

IN BOXED SETS

INDIVIDUAL BOOKS
Romancing the Spirit Series #1
Sadie's Spirit / Willow's Windfall
Cassie's Chase / Phoebe's Pharaoh
Vanessa's Valentine / Autumn's Angel
Romancing the Spirit Series #2
Carol's Christmas / Allison's Alibi
Gracelynn's Genie / Michelle's Miracle
Heather's Hero / Chloe's Cupid
Romancing the Spirit Series #3
Sabrina's Storm / Jenny's Justice
Stella's Star / Gigi's Gift
Phoenix's Phantom / Fiona's Freedom

. . .

The Christmas Collection

Dear Reader

I hope you enjoyed this book. If you want to know about future releases by CB Samet, you can CLICK HERE (or visit www.cbsamet.com) to sign up for my mailing list! I promise I won't spam you. I only send an email when I have a new book released, giveaways, or special discounts. And I'll never sell your information. You can also unsubscribe at any time.

If you enjoyed this story, kindly let others know by posing a brief comment on social media or leave a review where you purchased it.

Thank you for reading,
CB Samet

Other Books by CB Samet

Looking for more romantic suspense with more action and sizzle? How about with an urban fantasy twist? Check out my supernatural adventures...

The Shadow Guardians Trilogy

Urban fantasy Norse Mythology Adventure

Get *Raven's Flight, a prequel novella* for FREE. In my newsletter, you'll learn about me, special discounts, and new releases.

Raven's Flight, prequel novella

Raine Down, Book 1

Rosalyn's Run, novella

Storm Surge, Book 2

Anka's Orb, novella

Sky Fall, Book 3

Olympian Awakenings Trilogy

Urban fantasy Greek Mythology Adventure

Grab the prequel exclusively HERE.

Stone Hearts

Winds of Destiny

Flame and Shadow

~

The Rider Files

Romantic Suspense Thrillers

Meridian File / Masters File / Box Set 1

McMillan File / Maltisse File /Box Set 2

Storm File / Sullivan File / Box Set 3

Sharp File / Sizani File / Box Set 4

Rivera File / Rucker File / Box Set 5

Richmond File / Redwood File / Box Set 6

Atlas File / Angel File / Box Set 7

Buy 4book box sets direct from author and save 10%

Payhip. Use code E152M0GZG4

~

The Dr. Whyte Adventure Novels

Thriller Series

Black Gold

Whyte Knight

Gray Horizon

~

Love action/adventure and strong female leads in a fantasy world? Check out my other genre:

The Avant Champion Fantasy Series

The Avant Champion: Rising

Malakai: An Avant Champion Origin of Malos Story (prequel)

The Avant Champion: Honor

The Avant Champion: Ashes

Brothers' Bond: An Avant Champion Malakai Story

The Avant Champion: Conquest

Isabel: An Avant Champion novelette

The Avant Champion: Redeem

Sample Chapter

When attorney Jenny Wiley sees the ghost of a murder victim, her hunt for justice thrusts her into a world of secrets and danger. Can Jenny survive her hunt for justice, or will she be the next victim?

~

Jenny's Justice

"Why do you want to ruin a good thing?" he demanded.

A wave of rage surged inside him. How dare Cecilia try to blackmail him? Did she comprehend who he was?

He'd tried to reason with her, but the conversation had escalated to arguing, followed by threatening. They'd had a mutually beneficial relationship. He'd paid for her time and expertise. Now she was pulling this stunt?

They argued in her living room—a minuscule space with a small television and a couch that smelled like a perfume shop. He struggled to keep his voice low. No one could know he was there. He wouldn't have even come to this dump if she hadn't turned against him.

"Everybody gets mad. But everybody pays," the woman's pupils were pinpoint—tiny little beads in a sea of blue fire.

No wonder she was being so brazen. She was high on drugs. She'd told him her routine once: amphetamines in the morning, cocaine in the afternoon, sedatives when she needed to sleep.

She knew how to regulate the drugs she gave herself, and nights with her intoxicated made for a fun time. But this drug addict thought she was going to get away with blackmailing him? Not in his lifetime.

"Drop it," he snapped, the force of his words driving her backward and into the kitchen—another tiny room with bland white cabinets and cheap laminate countertops.

"I'm not paying you a penny. You think you'll ruin me? I'll ruin you," he said.

"What are you going to do?" Cecilia scoffed. "Send me to jail for drug charges? Been there, done that. I'll be out in a less than a month. I don't have anything to lose. You, on the other hand, have a career, a house—well, a couple of them—and probably wife number three in the pipeline. You have a lot to lose, so don't try to go head-to-head with me." She poked a long acrylic nail into his chest with each of the last several words.

He panicked as fury filled every crevice of his mind. He did have a great deal to lose. He couldn't let her get away with this. On primal instinct, before he understood his own actions, his hand closed over the handle of one of her kitchen knives.

And then there was blood. So much blood.

Jenny sat at the prosecutor's table watching the jury follow the defense attorney's every move.

He walked gracefully in his shimmering slate suit and spoke in a deep, authoritative voice like liquid satin as he began his opening statement. Like a fine, expensive bourbon—a burn so smooth you actually enjoyed it. "My name is Beaufort Montrose, but people call me Beau. Now, South Carolinians pronounce Beaufort as Bew-furt. Here in North Carolina, we say Bo-fert. To keep it simple, call me Beau."

Jenny suppressed an eye-roll. If she had a golden coin for every time she had to hear Beau Montrose talk about his name, she'd have a collection to rival her father's. And yet, the jury always melted into an adoring puddle at Beau's feet. Some combination of his impeccable hair, captivating blue eyes, confident stroll, and melodic voice lured them to his side. Of course, as the prosecuting attorney, she was immune to his charm.

SONG OF THE SIREN.

She scratched the words into her notebook with her black ballpoint pen. The smell from the ink wafted toward her.

What did she have to combat Beau's glamor? Her suit was from a mall department store and never seemed to look crisp despite her ironing. Her thick blonde hair was pulled back in a bun—because who had time for anything else? At least her bangs were even. Mostly. Her name certainly didn't have a movie star vibe like Beaufort Montrose.

The adoring jury watched Beau's every move as they sat in black high-back chairs behind a half wall of polished mahogany. Behind Jenny, the wooden pews were packed with spectators.

"Now, Miss Jenny Wiley here will try to convince you my client has broken the law," Beau continued eloquently. "But I ask you to carefully focus on the facts—and the facts only. Be careful not to confuse established facts with loose conjecture."

Truth, Jenny reminded herself. She had truth on her side. She reached into her pocket and rubbed the coin she carried as she glanced at the defendant.

Guilty.

She had the truth: the defendant had pulled the trigger and killed his employer. When Jenny walked the jury through events as they'd unfolded leading up to the murder, the jury would see the truth. No high-priced defense attorney—not even the best in Charlotte—could hide Bubba Hollins' guilt.

Work your magic, Beau. It's all smoke and mirrors.

Beau Montrose caught sight of the assistant district attorney leaving one of the judges' chambers.

He quickened his pace to catch up to her. "Fraternizing with the judge," he teased.

Jenny Wiley shot him a look of daggers without slowing her pace. Her heels clicked on the marble flooring.

Beau chuckled. She was fun to rile, and her reputation was so squeaky clean they both knew his words were weightless.

"Nice presentation this morning," he continued. "Although you wasted too much breath on a case I'll win."

"Not this time," she said.

He arched an eyebrow. "Such confidence."

Her tone of conviction was one of her tells—like a gambler; whenever Jenny insisted the defendant was undeniably guilty, Beau's job became an interesting, uphill battle. He felt a little giddy at the thought he'd be in for a challenge.

Jenny Wiley brought his acquittal ratings down—though he was still one of the most sought-after defense attorneys in the city. The damage to his record was mildly irksome but perhaps a needed dose of humility. She posed a challenge—an exciting call to action to be on the top of his game. And because she was a formidable adversary, the victory against her would be that much sweeter.

He glanced at her apparel. Her charcoal suit fit her slender figure nicely and revealed shapely calves. A faint ginger-orange fragrance wafted off of her.

"There are a throng of reporters out there," he mentioned mildly—a warning so she wouldn't be caught off guard.

She hesitated and touched her hair. The bun she'd started the day with had developed rogue fly-away strands, but they only added to her beauty.

"Miss Wiley, I wasn't suggesting you look unprepared. On the contrary, you look quite lovely," Beau said.

She frowned. "I don't like reporters."

"Allow me. I'm happy to address them first. See if I can calm them down before you address them."

She eyed him suspiciously as if wondering if he was playing her.

He wasn't manipulating her, but she was free to think what she liked. His job description was to impress clients with his bold brand and media show, not impress anyone in the DA's office. Some prosecutors disdained his flare but others understood the purpose of his theatrics. Sadly, Jenny had always unmistakably fallen in the disdain category.

"After you." She gestured.

He gave a polite nod before stepping outside. His smile widened. "If it pleases the press," he said to the crowd of reporters, "I can take just a few questions." He made a show of checking his watch.

All eyes focused on him. The volley of anticipated questions came at him.

"Do you have any evidence to refute the State's case?"

"How will you handle the witnesses who say they saw your client leaving the scene of the crime?"

After grabbing a latte, Jenny returned to her office to work on additional legal notes. She felt like she'd made a solid case against Bubba, but logic and truth didn't always prevail in the courtroom, especially when Beau Montrose was on the opposing team.

She acknowledged that her discontent with him stemmed from simultaneously admiring what an outstanding lawyer he was and disliking his peacock-display of strutting around the courtroom. His media antics added to her irritation, but that behavior was exactly what his clients wanted.

Her office was small, but she was one of eighty-five assistant district attorneys, so office space was always a negotiation and source of contention.

"Jenny," a voice greeted her at her door.

She looked up from her paperwork to see Stu Winslow, Charlotte's shinning District Attorney, standing in her doorway. Stu wore a gray suit over a white shirt and red tie. His black leather shoes had been polished to shine.

Despite his perfectly waved blond hair turning white, neighborly charm, and easy smile, his presence set Jenny on edge. Stu didn't appear in the doorway of an underling's office unless he wanted something.

"How are you, Stu?" She'd learned the hard way not to ask what she could do for him or why he was there when he spontaneously arrived at her doorway. If he wanted something from her, she wouldn't make it so easy.

"I'm doing well. I wanted to see how you're fairing after your opening remarks on such a high-profile case."

He'd been hovering incessantly ever since she'd been assigned lead on the Bubba Hollins case. She supposed the trial of the son of a congressman who'd supported Stu's election made him nervous. Since she wasn't an elected official, she didn't have a problem throwing her full capabilities into the case to convict a murderer. Stu had voiced his concerns about her being junior, even though she was part of the Homicide Team of prosecutors. She'd argued her track-record indicated she was ready.

When he hadn't backed her a hundred percent, Jenny

had refrained from reminding Stu of the many other cases she'd helped him prepare. When his success had been in some part due to her efforts, she'd been given no credit for her impact.

But that was okay; she was biding her time. All of the effort was part of office politics. She scratched his back; he'd scratch hers. When the time came for promotion or larger cases, more prominent cases, Stu would remember how she'd been a team player. He would remember, wouldn't he?

Reaching into her jacket pocket, she rubbed the coin, feeling the textured surface. "I've got wisdom, justice, courage, and temperance on my side. I'll be just fine." She had evidence also, but that didn't guarantee a win.

"That's good, because I watched Beau Montrose putting on a display at the press conference, and I didn't see you countering—reassuring the community that the killer would remain behind bars."

"I assure you, the killer will remain behind bars. I gave my statement after Beau. The media chose not to air it."

Stu smiled, somehow wide but not friendly. "Okay. Okay. These career-making cases are tricky things. They can also be career-ending."

Beau watched Jenny's closing arguments with interest. She'd prepared a precise summation, emphasizing key points in the trial without regurgitating all of the details to a saturated jury. She appealed to their analytical reasoning and not their emotion. Without straying from the facts, she kept her arguments concise.

Beau had represented his client as best he could—letting the burden of proof fall on the prosecutor. He'd raised credibility issues with witnesses, where applicable, and argued against small time-table discrepancies which existed.

But the prosecution had a solid case, and Bubba Hollins had been unwilling to plead guilty.

Jenny spoke with a soft voice, yet still commanded the room. She and Beau had been on opposing teams for several years now as he built up his practice in Charlotte, but he knew very little about her personally outside of work.

That probably wasn't going to change. Jenny was a straight arrow, no nonsense, no fraternizing with the enemy sort of person. And Beau preferred not to entangle himself in the type of drama that would befall him should he pursue the whimsical idea of getting to know Jenny Wiley.

When the session was adjourned to let the jury deliberate, Beau stepped into the hallway and checked his phone.

Five missed calls and three text messages.

He debated for a moment whether to respond to these now or take a few minutes to see if his client needed reassurance. Bubba had been mostly rude, arrogant, demanding, and demeaning throughout the course of this trial. Beau had enough self-worth that Bubba's behavior didn't bother him. He also understood that his clients were under a great amount of stress and their behavior wasn't always reflective of their true personality. However, he didn't think this statement applied to Bubba Hollins.

With that in mind, Beau opted not to play the role of

consolatory hand-holder but listened to his voicemail instead.

He stepped over to one corner by the window to avoid the crowd awaiting the jury's verdict.

"Beau, this is Karl." His cousin's voice sounded edgy and distraught. "This is my one phone call, man. I need your help. I'm in jail. Cecilia is dead, and they think I murdered her."

www.ingramcontent.com/pod-product-compliance
Lightning Source LLC
Chambersburg PA
CBHW021003150626
46549CB00012BA/1030